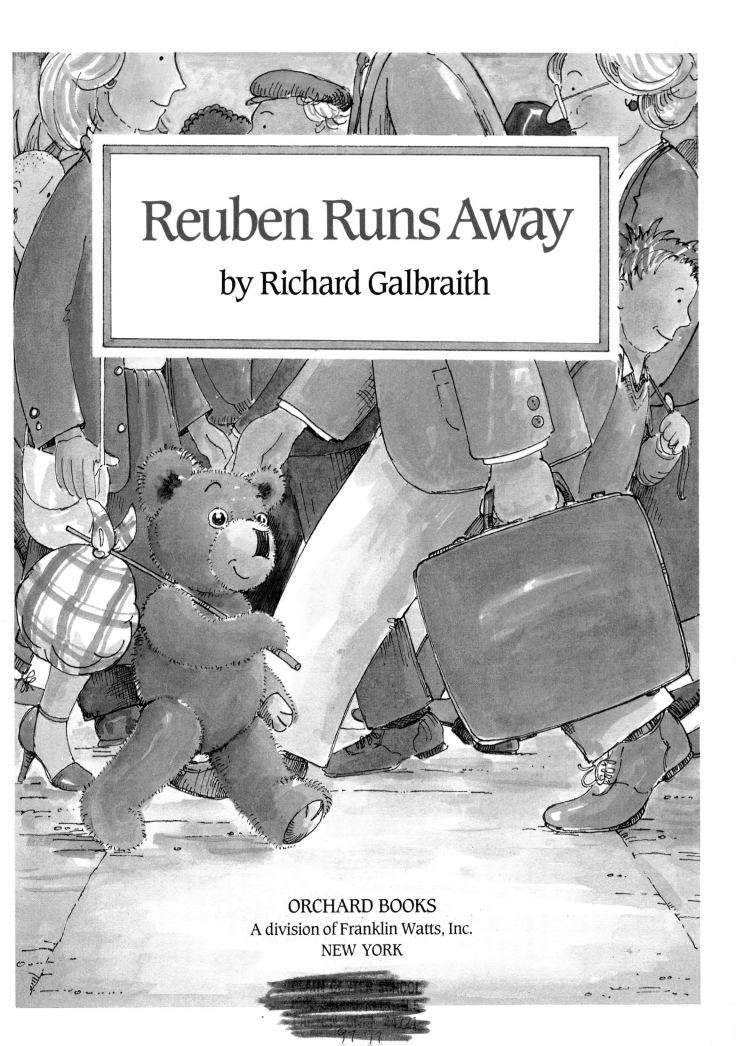

Reuben Runs Away
by Richard Galbraith

ORCHARD BOOKS
A division of Franklin Watts, Inc.
NEW YORK

To Dylan

Orchard Books
A division of Franklin Watts, Inc.
387 Park Avenue South
New York, New York 10016

Originally published in Australia by Greenhouse.
Printed and bound in the United States of America.
Book design by Sylvia Frezzolini.

The text of this book is set in 14 point Palatino.
The illustrations were done in watercolors, camera-separated,
and printed in four colors.

10 9 8 7 6 5 4 3 2 1

Library of Congress Cataloging-in-Publication Data
Galbraith, Richard, 1958-
Reuben runs away/by Richard Galbraith. — 1st American ed.   p.   cm.
Summary: A teddy bear named Reuben runs away from his rough
and active life with a girl and her dog.
ISBN 0-531-05790-9.   ISBN 0-531-08390-X (lib. bdg.)
[1. Teddy bears — Fiction.] I. Title.
PZ.G13037Re 1989   88-11741
[E] — dc19   CIP
                                                          AC

Reuben was a teddy bear. He lived with Anna
and her family and their dog, Raffles.

Although Anna loved Reuben, she did not always
treat him with care…

...and respect.

Sometimes life was downright dangerous.

Raffles was no better.

After one especially rough day, ending with eleven
stitches in his ear, Reuben had had enough.

He decided to run away.

Late one night while the family was sleeping,
Reuben packed his few possessions.

The next morning, the dew was still on the grass when
Reuben slipped out the back door and crept along the side
path. He made it through the front gate without waking
anyone.

He strode along boldly, thinking he might
try his luck in the city.

Reuben arrived at the railway station, asked for a ticket,
and found out what time the train left for the city.

When the train pulled in, Reuben hopped into one of the
cars and climbed onto a seat.

The train rattled and swayed as it raced toward the city.
"Do you mind if I read your newspaper?" Reuben asked
the man sitting next to him. But the man did not hear him.

Through the window, Reuben could see tall buildings,
chimneys, and cranes. Cars and trucks bustled along.
Smoke almost blocked out the sun.

Reuben felt very small in the city.

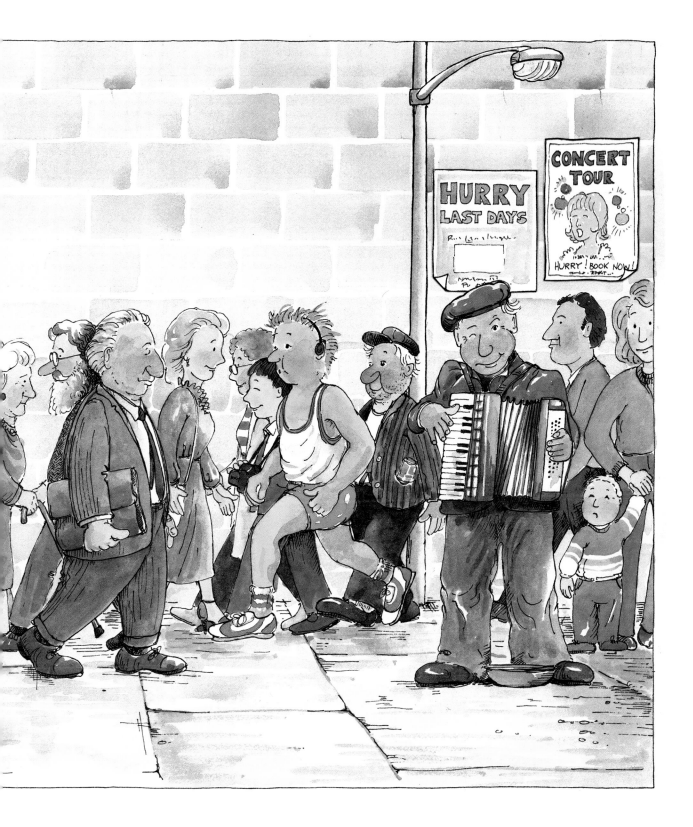

People hurried along and did not notice him, and cars
and buses honked at him when he tried to cross the street.
By evening he was tired and miserable.

Reuben saw people coming and going at the Grand Hotel.
It looked warm and inviting. He was sure they would
have a nice hot bath and a bed for him to sleep in.

But when he asked for a room, a very tall,
fierce man at the door said, "Bears are not welcome
at the Grand Hotel."

Reuben was so tired that he went around the
corner and crawled into a garbage can.
"I wonder if Anna misses me?"

CRASH! Reuben was jolted awake. He peered out of the
garbage can and saw the surprised face of an elderly lady.

"Dear me," she said. "You look far too good for the
garbage can." And she put him into a cart full of smelly
old bottles and junk.

She sold *everything* to a man at a second-hand shop.

Reuben sat with some toys that no one wanted anymore.

"What has a bear come to?" he asked himself.
But he was afraid to move.

Then, one morning Reuben was lifted from the shelf by a man with bright eyes and a big smile. "My granddaughter will like you," he said. And he tucked Reuben under his arm and gave him to…

. . . Anna.

Anna and Raffles now treat Reuben with the respect
a much traveled bear deserves...

...most of the time.